Confident Reader titles are ideal for c
greater reading confidence and stamin
read simple stories with a wider vocabu

Special features:

Wider vocabulary, reinforced through repetition

Detailed pictures for added interest and discussion

Simple story structure

Longer sentences

Ladybird

Educational Consultant: James Clements
Book Banding Consultant: Kate Ruttle
Subject Consultant: Ruth A. Musgrave

LADYBIRD BOOKS

UK | USA | Canada | Ireland | Australia
India | New Zealand | South Africa

Ladybird Books is part of the Penguin Random House group of companies whose addresses can be found at global.penguinrandomhouse.com.

www.penguin.co.uk   www.puffin.co.uk   www.ladybird.co.uk

First published 2025
001

Story by Ellen Philpott
Written by Abbie Rushton
Text copyright © Ladybird Books Ltd, 2025
Illustrations by Fran and David Brylewski
Illustrations copyright © Ladybird Books Ltd, 2025
With thanks to Child Autism UK and Pace

The moral right of the author and illustrator has been asserted

Printed in Dubai

The authorized representative in the EEA is Penguin Random House Ireland, Morrison Chambers, 32 Nassau Street, Dublin D02 YH68

A CIP catalogue record for this book is available from the British Library

ISBN: 978-0-241-67426-0

All correspondence to:
Ladybird Books
Penguin Random House Children's
One Embassy Gardens, 8 Viaduct Gardens, London SW11 7BW

Turtle Trouble

Written by Abbie Rushton
Illustrated by Fran and David Brylewski

Miss Zebra had a new book.

"Who knows what animal migration is, class?" Miss Zebra asked.

Tao Meerkat put a hand up. "I do!" he said. "It's when wild animals go to a new place."

"That's right!" Miss Zebra said. "Let's find out about ocean migration."

"Yes!" said Ali Lion. "I love being in the water."

Suddenly, the class were in the ocean!

"The water is so warm!" said Ali.

"Look at all the fish!" cried Tao.

Ali Lion swam fast through the water, laughing. He swam right into a turtle!

"Hello," said the turtle. "I'm Tilly."

"Where are you going?" Ali asked.

"It's migration time for me," Tilly said. "I'm going to the place where I hatched, so I can lay eggs."

"Can we come?" Tao Meerkat asked.

Tilly laughed. "It's a long way!"

"We could come a little way," said Ali.

"Yes, do that!" said Tilly.

They swam on. Then Ali asked, "What's that, Tilly?"

"A coral reef," said Tilly. "I eat seagrass near there."

"I see," said Ali. But Ali was not so sure about eating seagrass.

"Hello, Tilly Turtle!" said a fish from the reef.

But suddenly, the fish went to hide. Ali looked up.

"Oh no! There are sharks here!"

"Sharks?" Tao cried.

"We should hide, too!" Tilly said. "Here, come this way!"

They all swam after her.

Suddenly, the water went cold. Then Ali was pulled away into a fast current.

"Help!" he cried.

Tao was being pulled away, too. What was going on?

"Oh no! We are stuck in a current!" Tilly cried.

They were pulled this way and that way through the water.

"Hold on to me!" Miss Zebra said. But Ali could not.

Then Tao got hold of Ali's hand! The wild current pulled them this way and that.

"Hold on!" Tao cried.

After a long time, the current went away again.

"Are you all OK?" Miss Zebra asked.

"Just about," said Ali.

But Tilly was not sure.

"Where are we? This water is too deep!" Tilly cried. "I must go to lay my eggs in the right place."

"You will be OK," Tao said. "We can help you find the way back."

"Look!" said Ali. "It's the little fish from the coral reef. They will know the way."

"Let's go!" said Tao.

They went after the fish.

Just then, Ali swam into a bit of old net.

"Help me!" he cried. "I'm stuck."

Tilly and Tao got the old net off Ali.

"Thank you," Ali said.

"Who put this here?" Ali asked.

"People put their rubbish in the ocean all the time," Tilly said.

"That's not right," Tao said. "People should hold on to their rubbish."

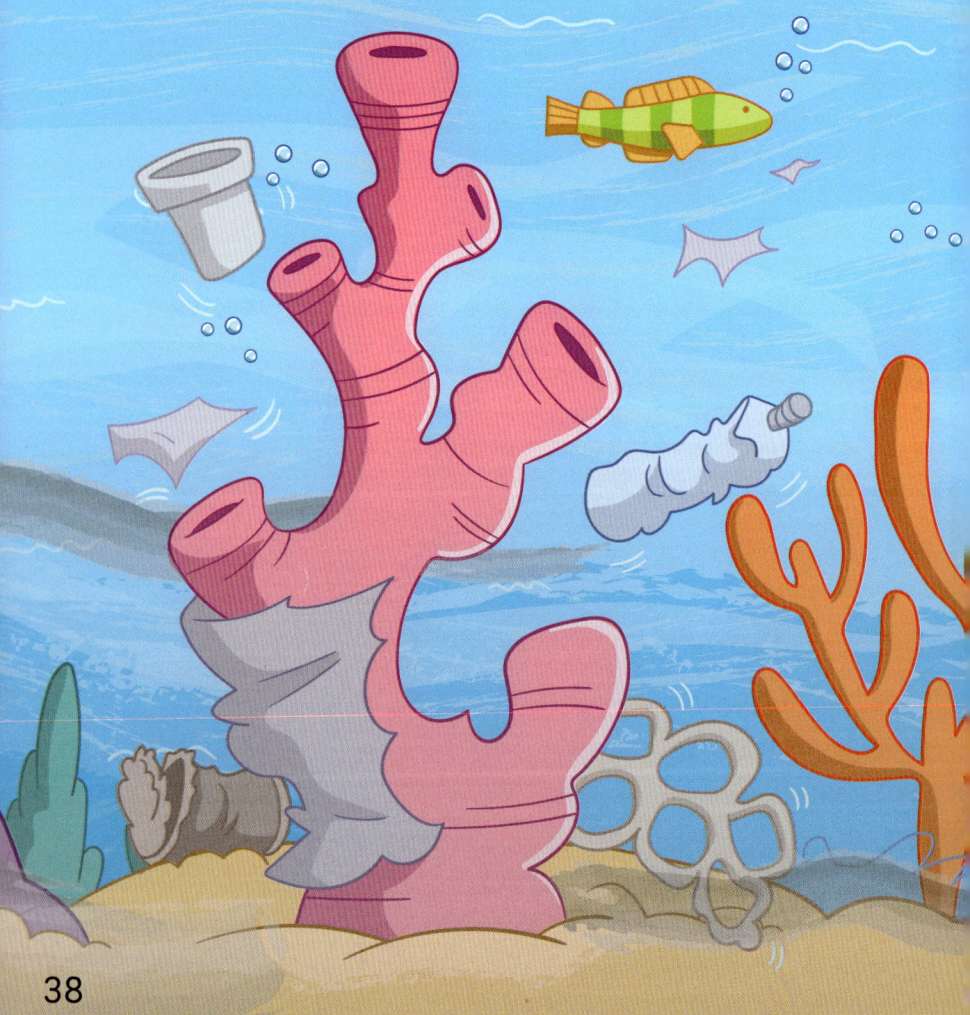

"Look! There is that little fish again!" Ali said.

They swam on a bit more.

"It's not so deep here, and here's the reef!" Tilly cried.

"Thank you!" Tilly said to them all. "I must go and lay my eggs."

Tilly swam off.

"Tilly will not see the little turtles hatch," Miss Zebra said. "After she lays her eggs on land, she will go back to the ocean."

"I loved the ocean!" Tao cried.

"That book was good," Ali said.

"But all that rubbish is not good," said Tao.

"We must do more to help the animals of the ocean," said Ali.

How much do you remember about the story of *Turtle Trouble*? Answer these questions and find out!

- Where is Tilly Turtle going?
- What does Tilly eat?
- Why does the fish on the coral reef hide?
- What does Ali Lion get stuck in?
- What will Tilly do after she lays her eggs?